from THE WOMEN'S PRESS

Angela Martin is a well known cartoonist. Her other cartoon book, *A Good Bitch,* was published by The Women's Press in 1984. She was a teenage werewolf.

ANGELA MARTIN

You Worry Me Tracey You Really Do!

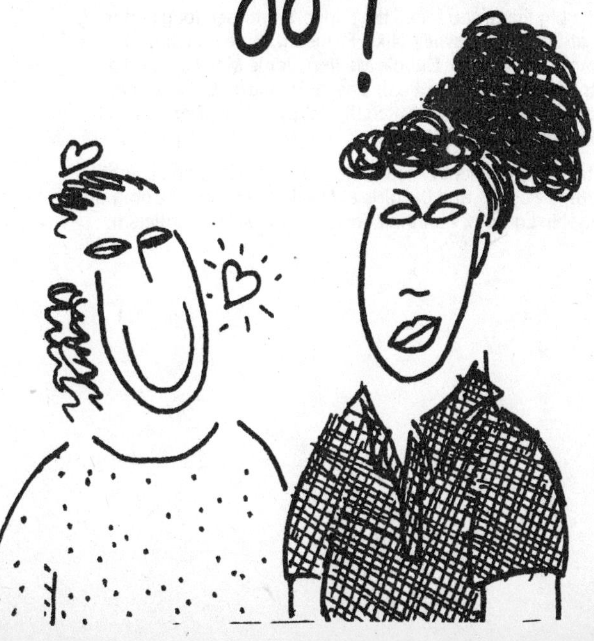

First published by The Women's Press Limited 1987
A member of the Namara Group
34 Great Sutton Street, London EC1V 0DX

British Library Cataloguing in Publication Data
Martin, Angela
You worry me Tracey, you really do!
1. English wit and humour, Pictorial
I. Title
741.5'942   NC1479
ISBN 0-7043-4902-7

Printed and bound in Great Britain by
Hazell Watson & Viney Ltd,
Aylesbury, Bucks.

Acknowledgments

Special thanks - especially for ideas, advice and inspiration to:
Janie Lawrence, Thea Hankinson, Christine Hankinson, Pam
Muttram, Sue Botcherby, Di Whittaker, Louise Whittaker, Mary
Curran and Ruth Curran, Julia Keenan, Melanie Keenan, Judith
Banbury, Beswick Girls' Project, Free Range Project Girls' Night,
(Whalley Range).

And a big thank you for all the support, interest, long suffering
etc. etc. to Sally Cawley, Nikki Pattison, Anne Kenyon, Ann
Inman, Julie McKay, Debbie Melling, Janie Morris, Maggie
Fortnam, Jacqui Greenfield, Sheila Stannard, Chris Vernon,
Linda Goodacre, Laura Mitchell, Nancy Jaeger, Patricia McErlain,
Rose Martin and Joy Wales.

Lastly many thanks to The Women's Press - Christina Dunhill,
Suzanne Perkins and the girls at North Westminster Community
School in London, - for their time, comments and criticism.

CRUSHES...

FAMOUS

CRUSHES.

HE'D BE QUITE NICE IF....

1	He shut up occasionally	
2	He changed his socks	
3	He lived in Australia	
4	He washed	
5	He was completely different	
6	He practised	

Should I?
or shouldn't I?
If, I don't
I might lose him
If I do, I might
lose him......

Look cleaner!
Look fresher!

what's her secret?

5 baths a day
no sweat glands
Garlic
Strong disinfectant
mints
clean socks

Oh Julie
I expect you've heard the rumours
I didn't really go with Craig
He only put his arm round me because I was cold
he's like that isn't he...?
I know it's none of my business Karen, but I think you're being really cruel to Craig.....

OK, we'll just be friends—

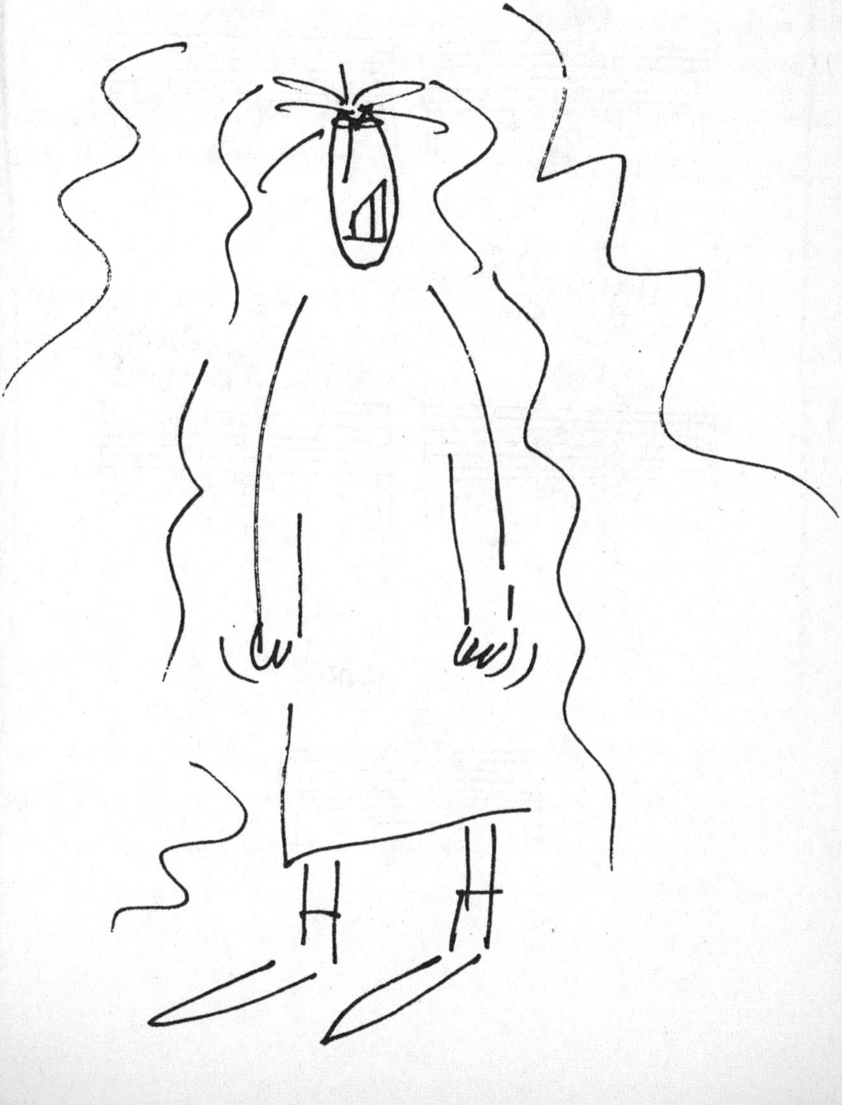

BREAKING UP IS SO
① HARD TO DO —

② Easy to do—

Freedom

The Green Light

What a RELIEF!

Life starts today

The chains roll off

YIPPEE!

BREAKING UP IS SO

③ mutual

MULTIPLE CHOICE
I don't want to go to the party because......
1 I don't want to see X
2 X will kill me
3 XY & Z will be there – and I've told them I'm going to W
4 I've got hairy legs
5 I've got spots
6 I'm too fat for my jeans
7 I haven't got anything to wear
8 Z will be there
9 Z won't be there
10 My dad's coming to meet me after.........

I'll be your best friend..

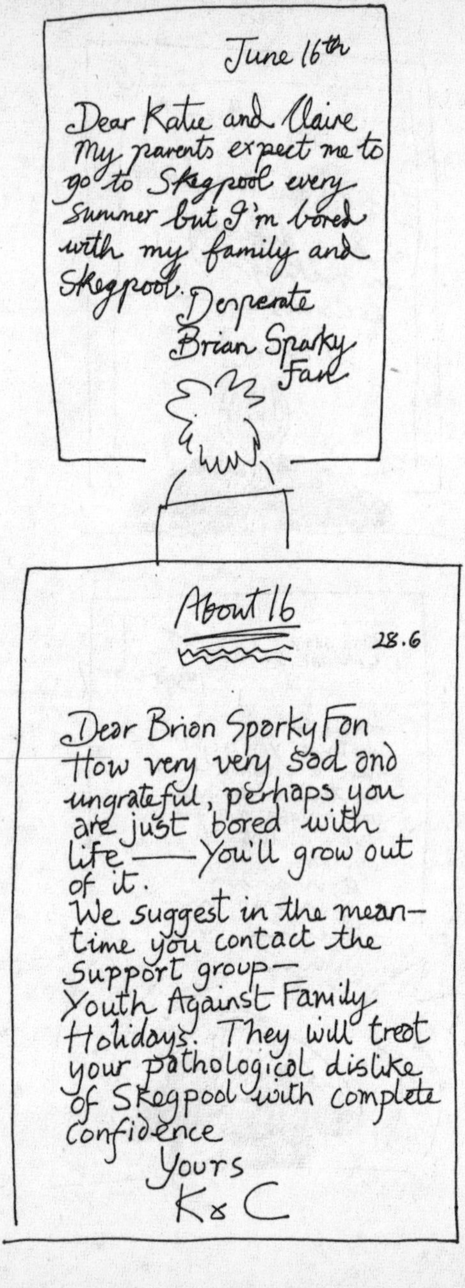

June 16th

Dear Katie and Claire
My parents expect me to
go to Skegpool every
summer but I'm bored
with my family and
Skegpool. Desperate
Brian Sparky
Fan

About 16

28.6

Dear Brian Sparky Fan
How very very sad and
ungrateful, perhaps you
are just bored with
life —— You'll grow out
of it.
We suggest in the mean-
time you contact the
Support group—
Youth Against Family
Holidays. They will treat
your pathological dislike
of Skegpool with complete
confidence
          Yours
          K & C

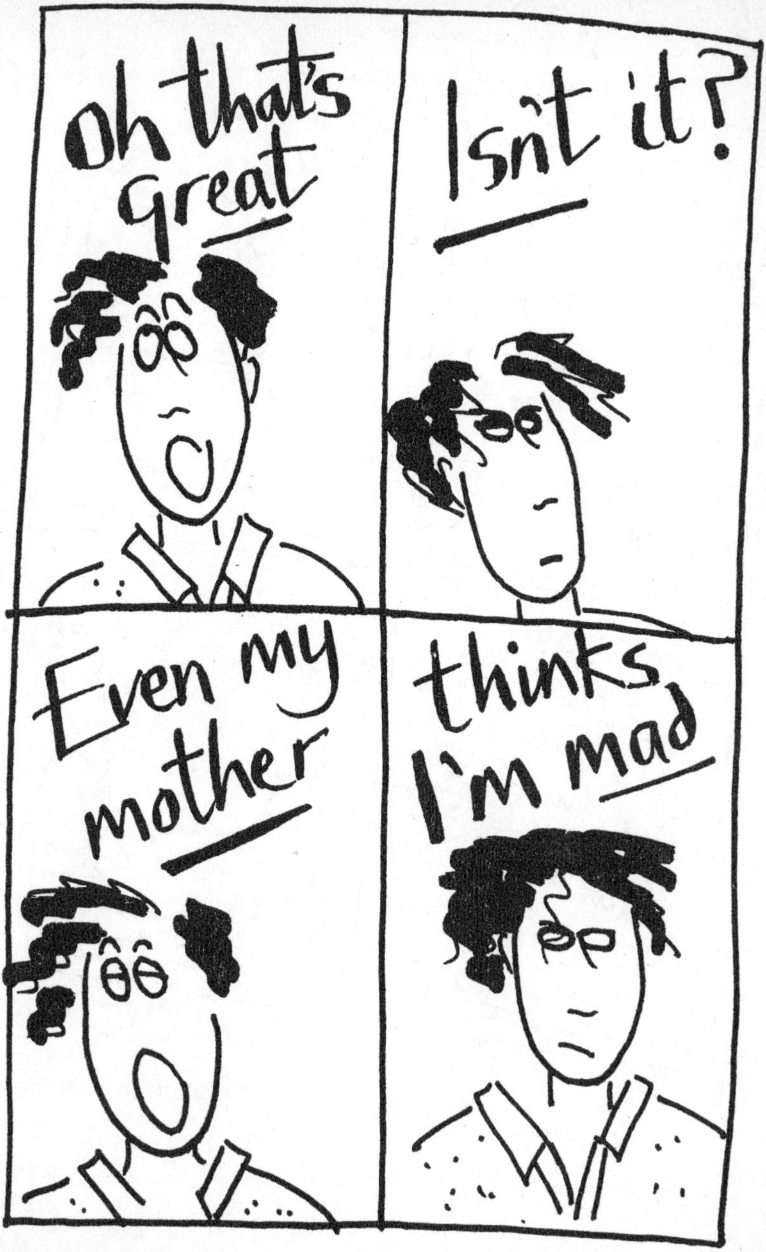
Oh that's Great
Isn't it?
Even my mother
thinks I'm mad

JUST SHOW SOME TOLERANCE
WILL YOU?
LIKE I DO
LIVING WITH WIERDOS
LIKE YOU
She used to be such a quiet girl

THINGS TO DO

PUT A 'FOR SALE' SIGN......

ROUND YOUR BROTHER'S NECK...

AND SEE IF YOU GET ANY OFFERS......

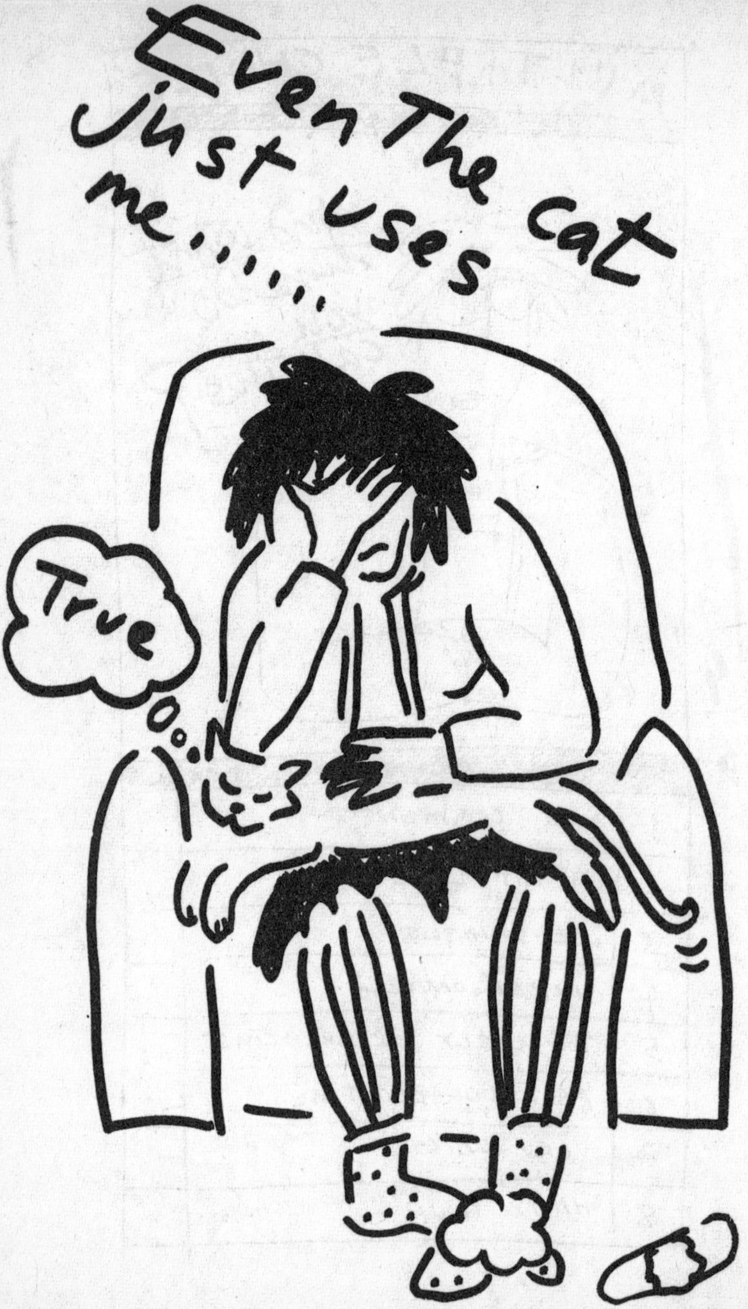
Even The cat just uses me......
True

Get the tea, put the twins to bed— homework— look after parents feed the cat— So much for wild youth!

Moods

EXCERPTS from
THE EXPERTS

THAT BEHAVIOUR
DOCTOR IN A GIRL
IS ABNORMALLY
ABNORMAL.

Apart from being bored...
I suppose I'm a misfit
Well.... That sounds interesting
No it's NOT it's BORING

My boyfriend is always telling me
He loves me
YUK
and I don't know why
But this puts me off....

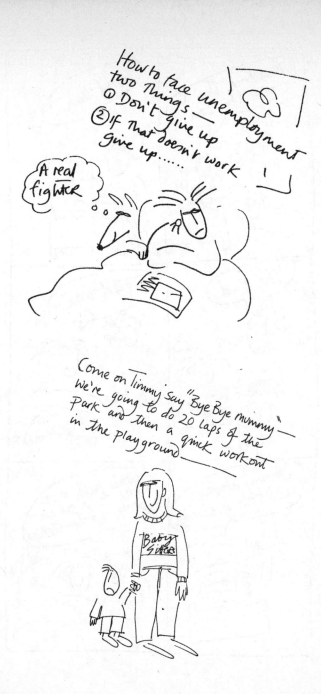

CINDERELLA

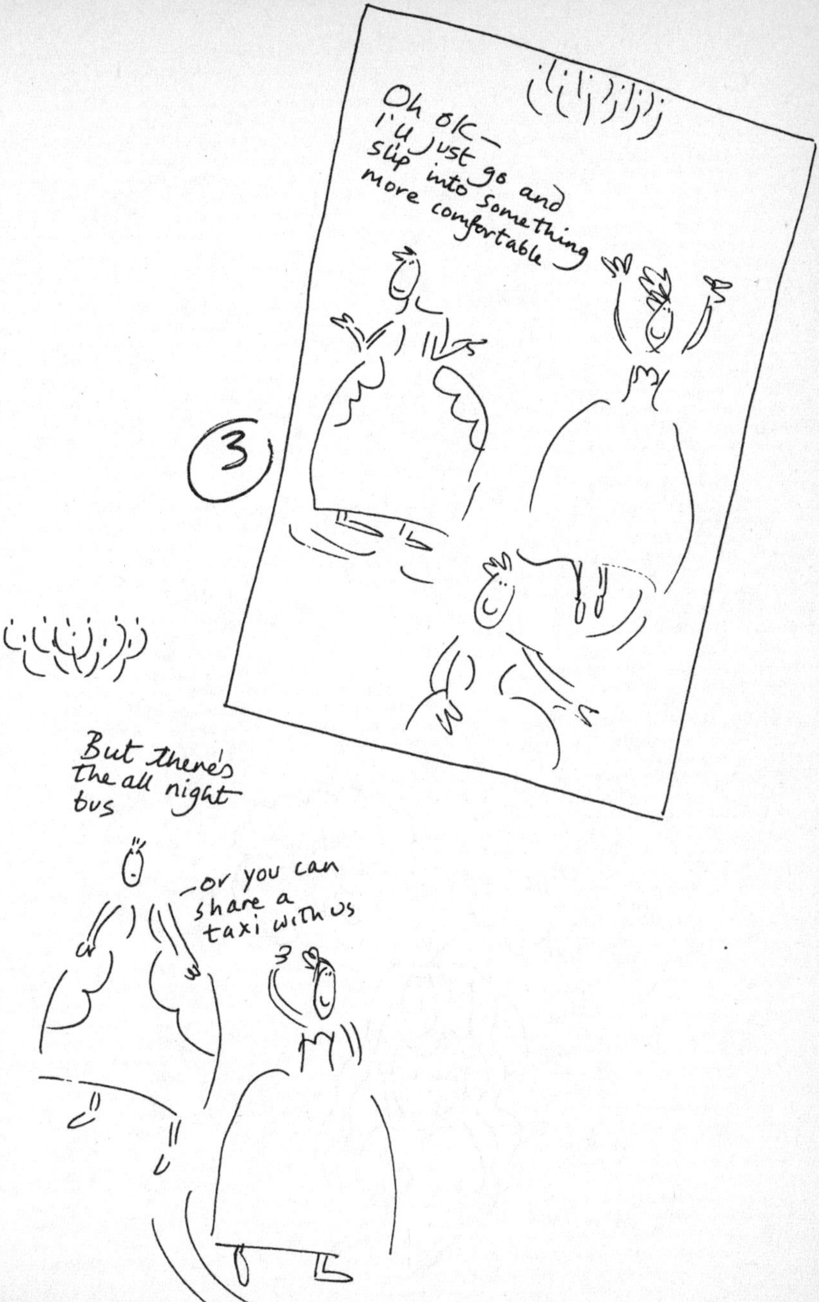

3
Oh ok — I'll just go and slip into something more comfortable
But there's the all night bus
— or you can share a taxi with us

Eileen Fairweather
FRENCH LETTERS: The Life and Loves of
Miss Maxine Harrison, Form 4a

Letters from Maxine to her best friend Jean, who has
left her to live in Lancashire. Max moans about the
unfairness of parents, and the meanness of older
sisters. But Jean and Maxine have a competition on –
who'll be the first to get a Real Boyfriend?... Max thinks
she's cracked it when she lands a dishy Parisian
penfriend.

THEN he says he's coming to visit... PANIC ! ! ! ! ! !

ISBN: 0 7043 4903 5
Fiction £2.95

Sandra Chick
PUSH ME, PULL ME

Cathy is fourteen and lives with her Mum. Then Bob,
Mum's new boyfriend moves in and everything
changes. Mum seems to care about nothing but
pleasing him all the time and she often gets angry with
Cathy.

Then Cathy's world falls apart. Bob rapes her and she
doesn't know where to turn for help. She just can't cope
anymore and starts to act up at school, even losing her
best friend Sophie.

Slowly, very slowly, her anger surfaces and Cathy
begins to work it all out.

ISBN: 0 7043 4901 9
Fiction £2.95

Kristin Hunter
**THE SOUL BROTHERS
AND SISTER LOU**

For Louretta and her friends, life in a black
neighbourhood of a large American city is hard, often
violent. Lou finds a place they can call their own; a
clubhouse, but it's hard to stay optimistic when one of
their gang is killed...

Making music makes life easier though, and as they
learn the true history of soul – the kids find hope for the
future.

ISBN: 0 7043 4900 0
Fiction £3.50

I've just been to a funeral
It was <u>DEAD</u> good.